QUEEN
VICTORIA'S
SWING

Collins
RED
STORYBOOK

Other Collins Red Storybooks by Karen Wallace

King Henry VIII's Shoes

Spooky Beasts Series
Gorgonzola's Revenge
Thunder and Lightning
Snapper Bites Back

QUEEN VICTORIA'S SWING

by KAREN WALLACE

illustrated by Chris Fisher

CollinsChildren'sBooks
An imprint of HarperCollinsPublishers

First published in Great Britain by
CollinsChildren'sBooks 1996

1 3 5 7 9 10 8 6 4 2

CollinsChildren'sBooks is an imprint of
HarperCollins*Publishers* Ltd,
77-85 Fulham Palace Road,
Hammersmith, London W6 8JB

ISBN HB 0 00 185663 4
ISBN PB 0 00 675219 5

Printed and bound in Great Britain by
Caledonian International Book Manufacturing Ltd,
Glasgow G64

To Rosie Llewellyn

Chapter 1

Amanda Benson stood in the middle of
Castletown Fair. Men in brown
knickerbockers wobbled past her on
penny-farthing bicycles. Girls in black-
buttoned boots, selling flowers, wandered
in and out of the crowds. "Lavender for
luck," they cried. "Roses for your
sweetheart!"

The tinkle-tonkle
music of a merry-go-
round burst into the air.
Amanda turned and saw
children in sailor suits
and straw hats rise
and fall on the
painted horses. ...

She stared at the horses' shiny black hooves, frozen in mid-gallop. It was almost as if time had been frozen, too.

A girl dressed in jeans and a T-shirt ran up to her. Clare Edwards' face was pink with excitement. "This is amazing!" she said. "I've never been to an old-fashioned fair! It feels just like the real thing!"

Amanda grinned and nodded. "There's a proper Victorian swingboat over there," she said. "Do you want to try it?"

"Why not?" Clare took her friend's arm. "How much money have you got left?"

Amanda felt in her jeans pocket. "A quid. What about you?"

"Same," replied Clare. "We'll have a ride on your swingboat and get an ice cream afterwards."

The swingboat stood on its own, away from the rest of the fair. It was wooden and fixed with metal rods to a big iron frame. Amanda had never seen a real one before. It was beautifully carved and painted with roses entwined with ribbons.

At either end was a picture of Queen Victoria. Written along the side in black curly writing were the words 'Queen Victoria's Swing. In honour of Wombwell's visit to Windsor Castle, August 28th, 1854'.

"I wonder who Wombwell was,"
murmured Clare.

A huge painted billboard stood in front
of them, with WOMBWELL'S written on
the top. It was a picture of a Victorian
circus and fair. An elephant pulled an
entire brass band on the top of a wagon.
Horses dragged cages of lions and tigers
while two clowns rode unicycles around

the crazy long legs of a young man on stilts. Behind them all stood the grey stone walls of Windsor Castle.

"Wow!" cried Amanda, still staring at the billboard. "See over there between the lions' cage and the tree?"

It was a swingboat. Just like the one they were standing beside. Clare looked around her. For the first time, she noticed no-one else was about.

"Who should we pay?" she said.

From the middle of the billboard a man in a striped waistcoat with a handlebar moustache stared down at them. He wore a glossy top hat with a W painted on it in gold. His grey eyes glittered fiercely in his face.

"Him," said Amanda with a laugh. "That must be Mr Wombwell himself."

There was an honesty box beside the swingboat. Clare dropped in her pound and the two girls climbed in.

At first it was difficult to get the swing moving, but after a while it began to sail backwards and forwards like a huge pendulum.

Clare closed her eyes. It was hot and the sound of the merry-go-round was a distant tinkle in the background. She fingered a silver locket that hung around her neck.

"My great-great-grandmother was a nurserymaid at Windsor Castle," she said. "I always wear her locket."

Amanda leant back and let herself fall into the rhythm of the swing as it went back and forth through the air.

"She was called Harriet," continued Clare in a drowsy voice. "She married a man called Tom. Their names are engraved on the inside."

"Mmm," murmured Amanda. "It must have been so different then. I wonder—"

But she never finished her sentence. Because at that moment, the swing slowed down and a brass band began to play *When Johnny comes marching home, today, hurrah, hurrah.*

Amanda sat bolt upright. A poster was

pinned to a tree in front of her. It said

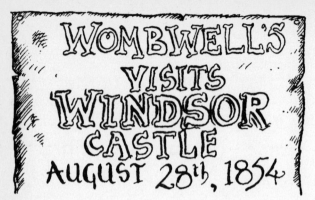

WOMBWELL'S
VISITS
WINDSOR
CASTLE
AUGUST 28th, 1854

Amanda rubbed her eyes and read it again. The words didn't change.

"Clare," she croaked. Her heart was banging so hard, she could hardly speak.

Clare stared wildly around her. "Where are we?" she said. Her hands flew up to her neck. "My locket! It's gone!" she gasped.

Then she saw the poster.

Chapter 2

It was as if the billboard had come alive. All around them the circus was setting up. Horses pulled animals' cages into a circle, while the brass band played on the back of an elephant-drawn wagon. The fierce-looking man in the striped waistcoat strutted about waving a cane. "This is a *royal* performance," he bellowed. "Anyone not doing their best will be soundly beaten."

Two clowns rode up on unicycles. "Where's Nelly?" said one. "The lions want feeding."

"She's on snakes, now," muttered the other.

"Who's doing the lions, then?"

"You are. Wombwell's orders."

"I ain't feeding no lions," shouted the first clown.

"Then find someone else to do it," replied the second, cycling off. "Hurry up, they're getting hungry."

"Duck!" hissed Amanda.

The two girls crouched in the bottom of the swing just as the first clown cycled past looking angrily around him.

"We must be in 1854! When Wombwell's Circus visited Windsor Castle, just as it

says on that poster," whispered Clare. "What are we going to do? How are we going to get back to our own time?"

"First things first," muttered Amanda. "If we stay here, we'll be made to feed the lions."

They peered cautiously over the side of the swing. Windsor Castle was only a couple of hundred metres away. "Let's take our chances in the castle," whispered Amanda.

Clare shook her head. "It's too dangerous," she said. "We might get caught."

"Let's risk it," replied Amanda. "I *hate* lions."

But Clare didn't reply. She was looking up into the square, curious face of a young man on stilts.

"My name's Tom," said the young man

with a big smile. "Don't worry, I won't give you away."

"We don't belong here," gasped Clare. "That is we don't belong in this time. You see—"

Amanda put her hand on Clare's. "My friend is trying to tell you that we're runaways. We're going to hide in the castle."

"I know," replied the young man. "I heard you talking."

"What do you want?" asked Clare suspiciously.

"I want you to do me a favour," said Tom. "And I'll help you in return."

"What favour?" said Amanda.

Tom's face looked honest and his eyes held hers without sliding away. Even so, it was almost impossible to know if they could trust him.

Out of the corner of her eye, she saw the clown still looking for someone to feed the lions. Amanda made a decision. They were going to need all the help they could get.

"We'll do it," she said, quickly. "What is it?"

Tom grinned. "I just *knew* you'd help me," he said. "Even though you look more like boys playing pirates than any girls I've ever seen."

He bent down and handed Clare a note.

Clare ignored his remark and stared at the grubby piece of paper. "What's this for?"

"The prettiest girl in the world is a maid on the first floor of the castle," explained Tom, his eyes going soft and dreamy. "She has bright red, wavy hair and the sweetest smile. She—"

"So you want us to give her this note," interrupted Clare impatiently.

"I do!" cried Tom. "And I will meet you back here just before the afternoon performance, at half past three o'clock."

"Clare!" hissed Amanda. "That clown's coming this way!"

Tom stood up. The stilts made him hugely tall. No wonder he could see in the first floor windows. He bent down to the swingboat again. "Listen," he whispered. "I'll distract the clown and you run for it.

There's nobody else looking." He winked and patted Clare on the shoulder. "Don't forget. Half past three, no later."

That very moment, the clown rode up to the swingboat. Clare and Amanda ducked down as low as they could.

"Well, if it isn't Spotty Herbert," cried Tom in a jolly voice. "Someone over there wants to talk to you. Something about

feeding the lions."

"I'm *not* feeding them," muttered the clown in a bad-tempered voice. "And don't call me Spotty Herbert."

Clare raised her eyes a millimetre over the side of the swing. The clown was halfway across the courtyard. "Now!" she hissed to Amanda.

The two girls scrambled over the side of the swing, jumped on to the ground and ran towards the shelter of a high green hedge.

For a moment, neither of them could speak, their hearts were hammering so hard. "Where now?" gasped Amanda.

Clare pointed to the door they had seen from the swing. "Hurry," she cried. "We must find some proper clothes or we'll be caught and sent back to that circus!"

"What game are the young gentlemen playing, McKenzie?" murmured a woman's voice.

Clare and Amanda froze. Then, as if in slow motion, they turned and found themselves a few metres away from a plump woman in a purple dress, sitting at an easel.

A smartly-dressed footman with a face like a bloodhound stood beside her,

holding a parasol to shield her from the sun.

He stared at Amanda and Clare and his dark eyes narrowed suspiciously. "Pirates, Ma'am," he said, in a low, cavernous voice.

The woman in purple peered once and returned to her painting.

"How delightful," she murmured. "I hope they will be changed in time for luncheon. It must be getting late."

All the while Amanda and Clare could feel the footman's eyes practically boring a hole in their trainers.

"What are we going to do?" muttered Amanda.

"Bow," hissed Clare. "Bow and run for it."

Which is exactly what they did. They dashed through a door into the castle, up a flight of stairs and found themselves on a small landing.

Below, the door opened. "Bessie," demanded the low, cavernous voice. "Where are the young gentlemen that came in this door?"

"What young gentlemen?" a woman squawked. "I ain't seen no young gentlemen. If you mean those princes, they be with their father in London."

There was a heavy tread on the bottom of the stairs.

Clare and Amanda tiptoed across the landing. Then they ran as fast as they could along the first corridor they came to.

"There's no point running down corridors," cried Amanda, grabbing Clare by the arm. "We've got to find some clothes." She turned and opened the

nearest door she could see and pulled
Amanda inside.

The room was gloomy after the bright
sunlight and it took a moment for the
girls' eyes to focus.

"We're in a bedroom," whispered Clare.
"Look at all those frills around the tables
and chairs. It must be a girl's room."

"Then there must be girls' clothes
somewhere," replied Amanda. She

crossed the room and went through a
door into a smaller room. It was a
dressing room.

The walls were hung with bonnets and
shawls. Petticoats were draped over
stands. There were bustles and corsets
and crinolines. There were smocks and
black stockings. There were morning
dresses and afternoon dresses, evening
dresses and night gowns.

Neither Clare nor Amanda had ever
seen so many clothes. "What happens if
we put on a nightie by mistake?" said
Clare, beginning to giggle nervously.

The giggle was catching. Soon
Amanda had tears rolling down her face.

"Or a bustle back to front," she
blurted. "Or a crinoline inside out."

"At least we know what to do with the
shoes," choked Clare, leaning against the

door and shaking with laughter.

Amanda lifted up a full, frilly petticoat and pulled it over her cut-off jeans. Then she took off her trainers and tied them round her waist.

"Just in case," she said. The laughter had gone from her voice. "And we'd better hurry up. That clock over there says it's almost one o'clock."

Clare was already trying on shoes.

Half an hour later, both girls looked completely different.

Clare wore a full, pale green skirt and a chequered jacket with a wide lacy collar. A pair of white kid-leather shoes fitted her perfectly.

Amanda had found a blue and white sailor dress with a big black bow in front. Her feet were a size bigger than Clare's, but she managed to squeeze into a pair of brown leather button-up boots.

There was only one problem left.

Their hair.

Amanda wound hers into a loose plait and held it in place with ribbons.

Things weren't so easy for Clare. She had short blonde hair. Ten minutes later, after much rummaging in a chest of drawers, Clare had a set of beautiful ringlets pinned to her own hair with flowers and bows.

They looked at each other in the mirror.

Two Victorian girls looked back them.

At that moment the bedroom door opened and a maid came in. She was a pretty young woman and her bright red, wavy hair spilled out from under her cap. She curtseyed, straightened up the bed,

picked up a doll that was lying on the
floor and walked out again.

Clare's face went the colour of wax.
She had seen the maid's face before. It
was in a faded brown photograph in a
silver frame on her mother's bedroom
table.

The maid's name was Harriet Armitage
and she was Clare's great-great-
grandmother!

Chapter 3

Amanda was halfway down the corridor before she realized Clare wasn't behind her. She turned and saw her friend stumble, white-faced, out of the bedroom.

Amanda opened the first door she saw and pulled Clare inside. They were in a child's room.

"What is it?" whispered Amanda. "What's wrong?"

Clare took a deep breath to steady her voice. "That maid is—"

"Who are you?"

Two girls stood in the doorway. The taller one strode into the room. She was wearing a maroon-coloured riding costume with full, laced sleeves and a black, narrow-brimmed straw hat. She pulled the hat from her head. Her long brown hair fell out of its pins and on to her shoulders.

"I am Princess Victoria," she announced in a haughty voice. "This is my sister, Princess Alice. What are you doing in our playroom?" She stared at Clare and Amanda. "How dare you wear my clothes!"

Clare stared back at Princess Victoria's wide face. She looked as if she was about fourteen even though the clothes she was wearing made her look much older.

Clare's brain spun like a kaleidoscope in her head. She knew that what they said now was crucial. Should they bluff or should they tell the truth?

The kaleidoscope turned once more.

Clare looked at Amanda. "I'm going to tell them the truth," she said quietly.

The playroom was light and airy with high ceilings. A little table and four chairs were arranged in front of a window overlooking the circus.

"I think, if we may, we should sit down," Clare said to the two princesses.

The four of them sat down whilst Clare and Amanda told their story. At the end, they pulled a net curtain to one side and pointed towards the swingboat.

Princess Victoria stared at it. Then she looked at Clare and Amanda. It was obvious she didn't believe them. She stood up and and walked across the room towards a bell rope that hung by the door.

"Wait!" cried Amanda. "I can prove it." She lifted up her dress and stuffed her hand into her jeans pocket. At the sight of the denim cut-offs, Princess Alice went bright red and stared at the floor.

Amanda felt the pound coin between her fingers. She pulled it out and held it up for the older girl to see. "Look at the date on this coin," she said desperately. "You *have* to believe us."

For a moment the room was completely silent. Then, Princess Victoria let go of the bell rope and walked back to where Amanda was standing. She took the pound coin in her hand. There was a picture of Queen Elizabeth the

Second and there was the date – 1996.

Suddenly Princess Victoria's face changed.

She believes us! thought Amanda. And she felt so faint she dropped back down in her chair.

"What a tremendous adventure," said Princess Victoria slowly, as if she was just beginning to understand what had happened. She looked at Clare and Amanda with amazement in her eyes. "But aren't you frightened?"

"Not yet," replied Clare, refusing to admit that she was scared stiff. "But we need your help."

Princess Victoria clapped her hands in delight. "Of course we'll help you, won't we, Alice." Then her voice became serious. "But our mother, Queen Victoria, must never know."

"Mama hates modern things," explained Princess Alice. "Or anyone who isn't respectable." She blushed. "Mama says they're dirty and have fleas."

"Who says we aren't respectable?" said Clare, stiffening.

Amanda put a warning hand on Clare's arm and grinned at the two princesses. "I guess it's difficult for you to understand," she said, calmly. "But so much has changed. In our time, everyone mixes with everyone else."

"And only dogs have fleas," added Clare, a little too quickly. Then she forced a smile. There was no point making things more difficult than they were already. How could these two princesses understand *their* lives, any more than they could understand the

princesses' lives, she told herself.
Besides, she had to find out more about
Harriet Armitage. Because, somehow,
Clare knew her great-great-grandmother
was the key to her and Amanda getting
back to their own time.

"Who is Harriet Armitage?" asked
Clare abruptly.

Amanda stared at her as if she was
mad.

"Who are you talking about?" asked
Princess Victoria, sounding puzzled.

"The maid with the red hair," replied

Clare. "We, um, saw her in your bedroom."

"Armitage is one of our nurserymaids," said Princess Alice, looking suspicious again. "Why do you ask?"

Clare's stomach turned over. If she told these princesses the connection, she might as well admit to having fleas and being unrespectable. And any promise of help would go out of the window.

"Our history teacher told us Victorian people had lots of maids," she bluffed, staring at her feet. "I was just wondering if that was true."

Princess Victoria and Princess Alice looked at each other and burst out laughing. "Everyone has maids," said Princess Alice. "We have dozens and dozens. Housemaids, lady's maids, laundry maids, nurserymaids..."

"And that's just upstairs," added Princess Victoria. "Downstairs there are many more. And butlers and footmen and—"

The sound of a gong suddenly reverberated through the corridor.

Princess Victoria pulled at a watch that was pinned to her riding costume. "That's the luncheon bell," she said. "We have five minutes before the second bell rings."

"Do you know how to make a formal curtsey?" asked Princess Alice. "Mama will not tolerate poor etiquette."

Clare and Amanda stared at each other. Neither of them had ever curtsied in their lives.

"Show us," said Amanda, quickly. "We'll probably need a couple of goes to get it right."

Alice stepped forward, moved her right foot to one side, smoothly swung her left foot behind it and bent low. All the time her back was perfectly straight. Then she slowly stood up again

Amanda tried it first. But her boots were too high and she lost her balance,

grabbed the edge of chair and fell over.

Clare managed to bend down but toppled over on the way up when her heel caught on her skirt.

The Princesses sat down on the little chairs, their hands over their faces, shaking with laughter.

The second bell went.

"What are we going to do?" asked Clare. Suddenly things didn't seem so funny.

Princess Victoria stood up and wiped her eyes. "Just bob," she said. She bent her knees and held out her skirts on either side. "Perhaps our mother won't notice. She's very short-sighted."

"Let's hope she's not wearing her glasses," muttered Amanda to Clare, as they followed the two princesses out of the door. "By the way, what's the sudden interest in this Harriet Armitage?"

At that moment, Clare saw the nurserymaid appear at the end of the corridor, her arms full of laundry. The princesses were already heading downstairs.

Clare felt Tom's note tucked inside her belt. A strange feeling washed over her: a strong and unmistakeable feeling that she had to deliver that note, *now*. There would not be another chance.

She turned and started to run down the corridor.

"Clare!" cried Amanda. "What on earth are you doing? You'll ruin everything!"

"Trust me!" said Clare. There was no time to explain.

Chapter 4

Harriet Armitage disappeared through an open door into an enormous airing cupboard. Clare Edwards stood, half hidden in the doorway. She had never seen so many shelves, each one stacked high with every kind of linen you could imagine.

With the oddest feeling, she watched her great-great-grandmother carefully put away the laundry she was carrying. She watched as the young woman smiled to herself and began humming a tune. It was the marching tune the brass band had played as the swingboat slowed down. Clare felt the kaleidoscope turn once more in her mind. It was all *so* peculiar.

There was the smallest tinkling noise. A locket on a silver chain fell from the nurserymaid's neck onto the floor. Harriet Armitage moved further along the airing cupboard, turned her back to the doorway, and bent down to gather a bundle of pillowcases from far back on the bottom shelf. It was obvious she hadn't noticed her locket fall.

Clare stared at the locket which lay open on the wooden floor. It was no surprise to her that it was the same locket she always wore around her own neck.

There was, however, one huge difference.

The locket that lay open was plain and shiny. There were no names engraved inside it!

In spite of herself, Clare gasped.

Harriet Armitage spun round. She opened her mouth to scream.

"Please!" begged Clare. "Don't!" And without another word, she picked up the locket and, with the note, pressed it into the nurserymaid's hand. Then she ran back down the corridor as fast as her white kid shoes would carry her.

"For the last time, *what on earth is going on*?" hissed Amanda. "We have two minutes to find the drawing room."

As they raced down the stairs, Clare explained as much as she could. "Don't you see," she gasped, as they stood at the bottom of stairs, "somehow, that locket and that message will get us back to our own time. The Tom on the stilts must be the Tom in the locket!"

Amanda shook her head. It was all beginning to get a bit spooky. What's more, she felt the whole thing was her fault. It had been her idea to ride the swingboat in the first place. She tried to make some kind of sense from what Clare had just told her.

"But how can you be sure it's the same Tom?" she asked. "There are thousands of Toms all over the country. It could be any of them."

A footman peered curiously at them from round a heavy oak door.

"I don't, for sure," whispered Clare. "But I *had* to pass on that message?"

"Why?"

Clare took Amanda by the arm and the two of them strolled sedately across the hall towards the waiting footman.

"Because if I hadn't, and that Tom *is* my great-great-grandfather, then the two of them must meet. Otherwise *I* couldn't exist."

Amanda's head was reeling. "Which means we couldn't get back to our time," she whispered slowly.

"Exactly," replied Clare, as the two of them walked into a huge drawing room. "But now that I'm pretty sure they will meet, I'll bet you that ice cream we were talking about that we'll be back in our time before the day's out."

Amanda looked round her. Even though it was bright outside, the drawing room was gloomy and lit with a flickering chandelier. Dark, heavy furniture filled every corner. And every table was covered with lacy cloths, framed photographs and china ornaments.

"The sooner the better as far as I'm concerned," muttered Amanda.

Princess Victoria and Princess Alice crossed the room to greet them. Clare was amazed by their self-control. But then again, she was pretty amazed by her own and Amanda's, too.

"We must introduce you to Mama," whispered Princess Victoria. "I have explained you were slightly indisposed after your coach ride from the country."

"What?" whispered Clare.

Princess Victoria shook her head imperceptibly. This was no time for questions.

Clare and Amanda followed the two princesses across thick Turkish carpets.

Beside a window sat a short, squat woman with the same full-cheeked face as her daughter. Her head was bent down over an embroidery hoop she held in her left hand. She had a long nose and her smooth brown hair was parted down the middle and wound in coils over her ears.

As the princesses approached, she put down her needlework and looked up.

Clare and Amanda went white. They had already met her. She was the woman in the purple dress who had been painting on the lawn.

"Oh, no," gasped Clare. Desperately,
she tried to remember if the Queen had
been wearing her glasses then. If she
had, they would find out soon enough.

The princesses curtsied and drew Clare
and Amanda forward. "Dear Mama,"
murmured Princess Victoria. "May I
present Lady Amanda and Lady Clare
Baverstock-Hextall, lately arrived from
Wiltshire."

It was all getting too much for

Amanda. A nervous giggle tickled her nose. She coughed and bobbed as deeply as she could without falling over. Even so, it was a near thing and, what's more it was a terrible effort.

Clare did a better job. She managed to pull off the formal curtsey, but then she was wearing kid shoes not button-up boots.

Queen Victoria picked up a fan and tapped it against her hand. "Step up, children," she said, peering at them. "Step up so I can see you."

Clare and Amanda stepped forward and nearly fell down with relief. Now they could see that the Queen wasn't wearing her glasses!

But the relief soon passed as both of them felt her short-sighted eyes burning through them.

Tap! went her fan.

"How you do slouch, Lady Clare," muttered Queen Victoria. "I must speak to your mother. A board strapped across the shoulders is the only remedy. Mark my words, you'll thank me for it."

Princess Alice nudged Clare's ankle.

"Yes, Your Majesty," muttered Clare quickly. "Thank you, Your Majesty."

Tap! went the fan.

"And you, Lady Amanda. Your hair needs attending to. It is lank and unkempt. A plait is an ornament in the right hands. Your lady's maid should be sacked."

Queen Victoria leant forward. "A patent shampoo of washing soda and olive oil would not go amiss, either."

Amanda needed no prompting. "Yes, Your Majesty," she murmured. "Thank you, Your Majesty."

But the Queen appeared to be getting into her stride. *Tap! Tap!* went the fan.

The entire room fell silent.

"The French," announced the Queen, pursing her little mouth, "have a disgusting habit of gargling at table."

She glared at her daughters. "No English gentlewoman should, in the slightest degree, imitate such gross behaviour."

"Yes, Mama. Thank you, Mama," murmured Princess Victoria and Princess Alice.

"Prince Albert, your dear father, is of the firm belief that the library of a dutiful wife should comprise of nothing more than a bible and a recipe book," declared the Queen. She looked directly at Princess Victoria.

Princess Victoria blushed. Even though she was barely fourteen, her father had already arranged her marriage to a Prussian prince she had never met. "Thank you, Mama," she murmured in a choked voice.

Queen Victoria turned her attention back to Clare. "What news of your father, the Lord Baverstock-Hextall. Is he well?"

By now Clare was so jittery, she felt an

over-whelming need to scream. The last time she had seen her father, he was washing the car and listening to a cricket game on the radio.

She dug her fingernails into her palms. "He, ah, enjoys the cricket, Your Majesty," she replied, bowing.

The Queen raised her eyebrows. "His Lordship must be well recovered from his fall," she murmured.

Clare went beetroot.

"The circus people are indeed colourful, Mama," said Princess Alice, quickly. "I have seen them preparing their performance from my window."

"Ah, yes, the circus," replied the Queen. She rang a small bell on the table beside her.

A second later, a footman appeared. "Ma'am?"

"What arrangements have been made for Mr Wombwell and his circus?" asked the Queen.

"Mr Wombwell and his employees dine with the servants as we speak, Ma'am," replied the footman.

Clare's heart banged in her chest. If she was right, at this very moment, her great-great grandmother could be talking to her great-great-grandfather for the first time.

The footman glided to the door and pulled it open. "A cold luncheon is served," he announced solemnly.

On the other side of the room, a carriage clock chimed.

It was half-past two.

As Queen Victoria walked slowly across the huge Turkish carpet, Clare and Amanda exchanged glances.

There was only one hour to go before the meeting with Tom.

Chapter 5

Amanda thought she knew what a cold luncheon was all about. At any rate, in her house, it was a slice of ham, a hardboiled egg, a lettuce and half a tomato. She didn't much like coleslaw.

So the sight of the dining room with the table and sideboards practically buckling under the weight of dishes piled with food stopped her dead in her tracks.

There were great silver platters of beef and ham. There were huge meat pies; cold stuffed game birds; endless bowls of vegetables and savoury jellies; and to top it all, a great wobbling brawn. "What's *that*?" whispered Clare to Princess Alice.

"It's called headcheese," replied the Princess. "It's made from a pig's head and feet."

"Yum–*my*," muttered Clare, sarcastically.

"Ssh!" warned Princess Victoria. "Don't speak unless you're spoken to. Mama will send you out."

Clare and Amanda took their places alongside one end of the table. Both of them were sure they would be stuck in this stuffy dark dining room for hours.

But they were wrong.

Queen Victoria gobbled her food as if she had a train to catch. Plateful after plateful was put in front of her. Forkful after forkful disappeared into her mouth. And all the while, she looked neither right not left, nor spoke one word.

So no-one else was allowed to, either.

Clare stared at the footmen and butlers, standing like statues around the walls. She remembered what she'd learnt about the Victorians at school. She thought of the army of servants that slaved away in the kitchens; that cleaned and swept, dusted and polished every day. What a life they must lead! Up at the crack of dawn every morning with nothing to look forward to but maybe an extra hour's sleep on Sundays and a couple of days off a year.

She thought of Harriet Armitage with her mountain of laundry and the endless shelves of bed linen. No doubt it had all been hand-washed, hand-squeezed, and pressed with a great, heavy flat-iron that had been heated up on the stove. Then there was the mending, the sewing and the cleaning of all those clothes they had seen.

Clare sighed and pushed her food to one side of her plate. Any life had to be better than that one.

At the other end of the table, the Queen laid down her knife and fork. All the way down the table, everyone else did the same whether they had finished eating or not.

A footman helped the Queen out of her chair and she glided out of the room like an Easter egg on wheels.

A fire had been lit in the drawing room. Clare watched as the Queen lowered herself into a comfortable padded seat beside the fire. Princess Victoria and Princess Alice stood beside their mother. As guests and not family, Clare and Amanda were escorted to a far part of the room near the door. No-one was permitted to sit down except the Queen. There was a silence while the royal stomach settled then the Queen spoke to Princess Victoria. Throughout the room, a babble of conversation nervously followed.

"The cholera epidemic is no better, I understand," said one man near to Clare. He had a bright red face with wispy side whiskers. "Bad air and overcrowding, I say."

"Too many beggars in London, the cause of it," added another man. "Send 'em to Australia, I say. Healthier for us

all, eh, what?"

"Send 'em to America, I say," said a
third man who looked like a badger.
"Telegraph cable's almost laid. Read it in
The Times, yesterday."

"America, Australia, what's the
difference?" muttered the man with the
whiskers. "There's no manners
between 'em."

"Infernal New Yorkers," barked a
granite-faced woman clutching a feather
fan. "Our exhibition at Crystal Palace

should put 'em in their place. Have you made an excursion?"

Both men bowed as introductions were made. "Indeed, Ma'am, I have," replied the man with the whiskers. "One of the seven wonders of the world, I'd say."

By the fire, Queen Victoria picked up her needlework.

Clare looked at Amanda. They had both learnt enough about Victorian etiquette to know that no-one would be allowed to leave the drawing room until the Queen was ready. And the Queen showed no sign of budging.

The carriage clock chimed. Clare spun round. It was fifteen minutes past three o'clock. There were fifteen minutes to go before their meeting at the swingboat!

The kaleidoscope turned in Clare's head. There was only one thing to do.

They had to get sent out of the room. She leant forward and whispered in Amanda's ear, then she took a deep breath and walked into the middle of the room.

"Knock! Knock!" shouted Clare, banging down a photograph on top of a little round table.

"Who's there?" yelled Amanda.

"Dummy," shouted Clare.

"Dummy who?" yelled Amanda.

"Dummy a favour and get me outta here!" shouted Clare at the top of her voice.

The room went completely silent. You could have heard a lacy tablecloth rustle.

In her chair by the fire, Queen Victoria puffed up like a toad. Her face was purple.

Beside her, the two princesses covered

their faces in their hands. It was
impossible to tell whether they were
hiding laughter or embarrassment,
thought Clare, much later. And sadly,
they would never know.

Thwack! The Queen picked up a cane
and broke it over the arm of her chair.
"Out!" she ordered in the coldest,

angriest voice Clare and Amanda had ever heard.

The heavy oak door swung open. Through the window, the first notes of a marching tune floated into the room.

When Johnny comes marching home, today, hurrah, hurrah.

Clare and Amanda turned and ran out of the door. There was no time to lose!

Chapter 6

"Hurry!" cried Clare. "Let's go through a side door."

They ran down the hall, but every door they tried was locked.

Behind them, an imperious voice shouted from the drawing room. "Find them and lock them up in their bedroom!"

Amanda rattled the doorknob of the last door. It was locked too. They were trapped. Now, there was no way to go except back, and that meant straight into the army of servants who chased after them.

Suddenly they saw their escape route – a small corridor leading off the hallway.

They ran round the corner and found themselves at the bottom of a small circular staircase. Harriet Armitage stood at the top. Her face was ashen and her hands

clutched the banister rail as if she was going to faint.

"Help us," begged Amanda in a cracked voice. "Please help us."

Clare stared into her great-great-grandmother's terrified eyes. "Take us to Tom!" she demanded. "He is waiting for us as well."

It was as if a spell was broken. The nurserymaid beckoned them up. "Don't ask no questions," she said in a strangled voice. Then without another word, she turned and raced down the corridor.

"She's taking us back to the playroom," gasped Amanda as they stumbled after her, holding up their skirts as best they could. "We'll be trapped."

"No, we won't," cried Clare. The kid shoes were pinching her feet horribly. "We have to trust her. It's the only chance we have."

Behind them came the pounding of footsteps running up the stairs.

"They're on the first floor," shrieked a voice. "Disgraceful hussies. They need a sound beating."

Ahead, Harriet Armitage pulled open a door and disappeared inside. Clare and Amanda ran after her.

They were in the bedroom where they had first found the clothes. It seemed like years ago, now.

Harriet Armitage pulled back the curtain. Whatever she saw made her tear off her cap, pull off her apron and climb out of her uniform as fast as she could.

Footsteps sounded at the end of the corridor.

"Try every room. They must be hiding in one of them."

Clare tiptoed back to the door, turned
the key in the lock and wedged a chair
under the knob. By the window,
Amanda's sailor dress lay in a crumpled
heap; her petticoat was chucked over a
chair; and one buttoned-up boot leant
drunkenly against a lamp.

"Hurry!" gasped Amanda. "Get out of

those stupid clothes!"

Clare stumbled towards her, tearing off her jacket and yanking down her full green skirt. She kicked off the white kid shoes, and elbowed her way out of her lacy white blouse.

Heavy fists banged on the door.

Outside the window, the brass band was tuning up. Rehearsals were over. The performance was starting in one minute.

Clare's hands were shaking uncontrollably as she tied up her trainers. She looked up at Amanda with crazy, round eyes. "We must be in that swingboat to get home," she sobbed. "I *know* we must!"

The balcony door opened.

Amanda and Clare stared open-mouthed as Harriet Armitage, dressed in her own clothes, appeared to step off the edge into thin air.

Amanda stumbled towards the window, then started to sway. "I think I'm going to faint," she said in a hoarse whisper.

"No you're not!" shouted Clare. A pitcher of water stood on the bedside table. She cupped both hands and filled them with water. Then she threw it in Amanda's face.

The door cracked open behind them.

As Clare dragged Amanda to the balcony, Tom appeared in front of them. "Cor!" he cried. His face was flushed and edgy. "In the nick of time, you are!"

Then he grabbed a girl under each arm. For a split second the ground spun dizzily underneath them. Now it was Clare's turn to feel faint. She groaned and closed her eyes.

The next second they were sitting on the wooden boards in the swingboat!

The bandleader raised his baton.

"Swing, Clare, swing!" screamed Amanda.

Clare looked up for the last time into Tom's square, honest face. "You're my great-great-grandfather," she whispered.

"I can't hear you!" cried Tom, cupping a hand over his ear.

"Thank you," cried Clare. "Thank you for helping us."

Tom grinned shyly. "You helped me," he said. "More than you'll ever know." He blushed. "Her and me, we're—"

"I know! I know!" shouted Clare. As she spoke, she thought her heart would burst in her chest. Then she squeezed her eyes shut again and swung forwards and backwards as hard as she could.

The band struck up with their opening tune. *When Johnny comes marching home, today, hurrah, hurrah!*

Slowly the swingboat began to move. Higher and higher and higher. Soon it was sailing through the air like a huge pendulum.

Amanda fell back. "Don't open your eyes," she muttered, as she let herself be taken away by the rhythm of the swing.

Around them the air was hot. They
seemed to be swinging for ages and
ages.

* * *

In the distance came the tinkle-tonkle sound of a merry-go-round.

Clare felt around her neck. Her silver locket was hot and sticky against her skin. The swingboat slowed down and rocked gently on its frame.

"Oi!" cried a voice. "You stopping all day or what?"

Clare and Amanda opened their eyes and looked down.

Two boys in leather jackets and baseball caps were glaring at them. "You've been in that thing for hours," said one. "What about someone else having a go?"

"Help yourself," replied Clare, climbing out.

"But watch out for the lions."

"What?"

"They need feeding," explained Amanda. "And the clown says they're hungry."

The boys exchanged pained glances and jumped into the swing. "Too much sun, I reckon," muttered one to the other.

But neither Clare nor Amanda were listening. They were staring at the huge painted billboard; particularly at the space between the lions' cage and the tree, just underneath a first-floor balcony of Windsor Castle.

The swingboat had disappeared!

Amanda reached into her pocket and pulled out her pound coin. "Fancy an ice cream?" she said.

"You bet," replied Clare.

"No, *you* bet," said Amanda. "In the big hallway, don't you remember?"

Clare fingered the locket she always

wore around her neck. "Amanda—" she
began slowly.

Amanda put her finger to lips. "Too
much sun, I reckon," she said.

Clare smiled and took her friend by the
arm.

They walked back across the field to
the tinkle-tonkle sound of the merry-go-
round and the shiny black hooves of the
painted horses, frozen in mid-gallop
forever.